Dear Reader,

Krystle and I hope you are enjoying the Little Rhino books!

Sometimes in baseball, a player will get injured and have to miss games. It takes a lot of patience to sit out while you're getting better. You have to take care of your injury. It's important to make sure that you are completely healed before you return, otherwise you could hurt yourself again. But even though you're injured, you can still contribute. It's important to support your teammates both on and off the field.

I've had a few injuries in my career. Every time, I just wanted to get back on the field. But I knew that it could make my injury worse. So I listened to my doctors, worked hard to get healthy, and before I knew it, I was back playing first base. My teammates appreciated the cheers I gave them while I sat on the bench. It made me realize that even though I wasn't playing in the games, I was still a valued teammate.

Krystle Howard

LITTLE Rhino

by **RYAN HOWARD**
and **KRYSTLE HOWARD**

BOOK THREE
DUGOUT HERO

SCHOLASTIC PRESS/NEW YORK

To the readers and fans of Little Rhino.

—R.H. & K.H.

ISBN 978-0-545-67497-3

12 11 10 9 8 7 6 5 4 3 2 1   15 16 17 18 19

Printed in the U.S.A.   113
First printing 2015
Book design by Christopher Stengel

· CHAPTER 1 ·
Tough Breaks

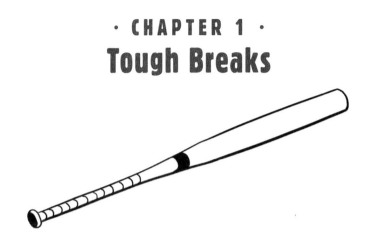

The pitcher looked worried. Little Rhino was sort of nervous, too, but he was ready. Butterflies were part of baseball! He blew out his breath and stepped into the batter's box.

Rhino felt sweat trickling down his neck. The air was warm and still. *This pitcher knows I can hit,* he thought. *It's me against him.*

The game was tied. Rhino's teammate Cooper had reached second base, and he would score if Rhino got another hit. With two outs, the game was riding on Rhino.

"Bring him home!" came a shout from the Mustangs' dugout.

"Strike him out!" came a call from the other side of the field.

Rhino watched the first pitch go by. It was way outside. He stepped back and wiped some dirt from the knee of his baseball pants. That was from sliding into third a couple of innings ago with a triple.

This pitch, he thought. *This is the one!*

The pitcher threw a fastball. It was low but straight down the middle. Rhino pulled back his bat and swung hard. The ball hit the catcher's mitt.

He felt a pop, but it wasn't his bat hitting the ball. A sharp pain surged through Rhino's right ankle. He fell to the dirt and winced.

"Yow!" Rhino yelled. The umpire called time out and Coach Ray ran from the dugout.

Rhino tried to get up, but his coach told him to stay still. He gently grabbed Rhino's right ankle. "Here?" he asked.

Rhino nodded. He blinked his eyes and bit down on his lip. It hurt, but Rhino tried to fight off the pain. "I'll be okay," Rhino said. He reached for his bat.

"I think you're done for today," Coach Ray said.

"I'm all right," Rhino replied. He flexed the ankle to show his coach that it was okay. "See?" But it did hurt.

"That's a good sign that you can move it, but it will probably start to swell," Coach said. "Let's get some ice on it."

Coach and the umpire helped Rhino to the dugout. They wrapped an ice pack on the ankle and propped Rhino's foot up on a couple of sweatshirts.

"Tough break," said Rhino's teammate Bella. She shook her dark ponytail and looked concerned. Bella was Coach Ray's daughter, and she had become a good friend to Rhino.

"It better *not* be a break," Rhino said. He didn't see what the big deal was. He thought he could have continued batting.

I get little bumps and bruises all the time, Rhino thought. *They never slow me down.*

After the third out, the Mustangs ran back onto the field. They hadn't scored, so the game was still tied. Coach sent Paul to first base to replace Rhino. Paul had played there early in the season, but he had a hard time fielding throws. Rhino had moved from center field to first base at the start of the season, and he'd done very well at the new position.

Paul and Rhino were the only left-handed players on the Mustangs. A lot of major league coaches liked to put lefties at first base. They could reach their gloves a little farther if a wide throw was headed toward right field.

Rhino smiled as his grandfather stepped into the dugout.

"How does it feel?" Grandpa James asked. He patted Rhino's shoulder.

Rhino shrugged. "The ice is making it numb," he said. "It doesn't seem too bad."

"We'll drive over to the hospital to get it checked out," Grandpa said.

"Can we wait until the game is over?" Rhino wanted to see his team win.

Grandpa raised his bushy eyebrows and laughed. "I guess so. I know how important your team is for you."

Things weren't looking good for the Mustangs, though. The Sharks had a runner on third base. If she scored, the game would be over.

"Come on, Dylan!" Rhino shouted. The Mustangs' pitcher was very good, but he was in a tight spot. Even a long fly out would bring in that runner.

The batter hit a sharp grounder to Cooper at shortstop.

Easy out, Rhino thought.

Cooper scooped up the ball and fired it to first base. The throw was high and slightly off target, but Rhino would have had no trouble catching it.

Paul wasn't as skilled, though. He stumbled as he lunged for the ball, and it bounced off his glove. The runner from third sprinted home and scored the winning run.

That hurt even more than Rhino's ankle. He would have made the play. Sitting in the dugout had cost his team the game. *If only I could be out there playing.*

"Now *that* was a tough break," Rhino said as Bella joined him on the bench.

Bella shook her head sadly.

"Good game today," Coach Ray said as the team gathered in the dugout. "Keep your spirits up. Let's go over and congratulate the winners."

Rhino stayed on the bench. He noticed Paul standing by himself near the dugout fence. Paul had his head down. Sweat was dripping from his curly red hair.

"Forget about it," Rhino said. "We all make errors, Paul. It's part of the game."

Paul frowned, but he nodded. "Thanks," he said softly. "Hope you get better quickly."

Grandpa James pulled his car close to the dugout. He helped Rhino to the front seat and drove to the hospital.

"It's not an emergency, but I don't want to wait until Monday to have that ankle checked," Grandpa said.

"The sooner, the better," Rhino agreed. He took a big swallow from his water bottle. "Whatever's wrong, I want to get it fixed. We have practice on Tuesday!"

Grandpa smiled. "I think you might have to miss that one," he said. "Ankles are tricky. They take awhile to heal."

We'll see, Rhino thought. His thinker told him he might need to be patient, but he was already hungry for more baseball. He'd been hitting the ball hard, and his team was winning most of its games. His first real baseball season was even more exciting than he'd hoped it would be. Just missing one practice would be a disappointment.

The ankle was feeling stiff from the ice and he couldn't put a lot of pressure on it. *I'll tough it out,* Rhino thought as they arrived at the hospital. *One little injury won't keep me on the bench.*

· CHAPTER 2 ·
Bottled Up

Rhino sat on a table in the hospital emergency room. He was still wearing his baseball uniform and his blue cap with the big white *M*. His right foot was bare, but his cleats and his dirty sock were on the other.

A friendly young doctor patted Rhino's toes. She told him that injuries like this one were very common.

"Ryan, you're lucky," the doctor said. "You just twisted the ankle joint a little. It's a mild strain."

"Can I go to practice on Tuesday?" Rhino asked.

The doctor shook her head. "Only to watch. No baseball for about ten days."

Rhino gulped. That meant he'd miss the next game, too. "Doc, are you sure?"

"You could make the injury worse if you try to play too soon," the doctor said. She told Rhino and Grandpa James to keep icing the ankle regularly for three days. She said Rhino should walk on it and do some easy stretching.

For most of the weekend, Rhino sat on the living room couch with his right foot propped up. A bag of frozen peas kept the ankle from swelling much. Rhino did everything the doctor had told him to do. But he was frustrated.

I need to mo-oo-oove, he thought. *Sitting around all day is boring!*

Usually, Rhino was always active, even on days when he didn't have practice or a game. He'd play one-on-one basketball with Cooper, or hit baseballs in the backyard with his older brother, C.J., and Grandpa. They were a busy family.

Sitting on the couch made Rhino feel like he had ants in his pants. All weekend, he read books and magazines and listened to music. He flipped through a hundred TV channels but nothing was on.

Rhino completed all of his homework and reading assignments for the week. He even did an extra credit project. He walked slowly around the yard, and he tossed a baseball into the air a million times and caught it. He was itching to run.

Rhino needed to keep icing his ankle on Monday, so he stayed home from school. Grandpa James took the day off from work.

In his mind, Rhino played baseball and basketball and football. He sprinted and leaped and caught and threw. But in reality, he stayed mostly on the couch.

By that afternoon, Rhino was very restless. There wasn't anything to watch on TV during the day. He'd read a book about dinosaurs, three more books about the planets, and another about his baseball hero Hank Aaron, who was a great home run hitter like Rhino wanted to be. But reading about baseball wasn't cheering him up the way it usually did. So he was glad to see his friends Cooper and Bella, who came over after school to deliver his homework.

"Just math and spelling," Cooper said, placing two books on the table by the couch. "Mrs. Imburgia says she hopes you're feeling better." She was their third-grade teacher. Bella was in a different class in the same school.

Cooper was dressed in a short-sleeved polo shirt. "Think you'll be back in school tomorrow?"

"Definitely," Rhino said. "My ankle's getting better already." He showed them that it wasn't swollen much, but there was a small purple spot where it was bruised.

"Will you need to use crutches?" Bella asked.

"Nope." Rhino explained that he'd be wearing

a thin, stretchy sleeve over his ankle, but walking on it would not be a problem. The sleeve would help keep the ankle stable.

"I'm supposed to walk," Rhino said. "I just shouldn't run or jump yet."

Bella pointed to Rhino's books about the planets. "We talked about Neptune and Jupiter at lunch today," she said excitedly.

"Really?" They were all in a group that met in the cafeteria to talk about their favorite subjects. The talk was usually about dinosaurs. Rhino and Cooper had been joining them for about a month now.

"What happened to T. rex and the stegosaurs?" Rhino asked.

"We decided to switch to astronomy this week," Bella replied. "We'll get back to dinosaurs soon."

Rhino sighed. Astronomy was the only topic he liked more than dinosaurs. He would have loved to have been part of that discussion.

"Too bad you missed it," Cooper said.

"Yeah," Rhino said with a sneer. "Too bad."

"We'll be talking about Venus and Mars tomorrow," Bella said. "So study up."

Rhino brightened. He'd learned a bit about those planets today. "Venus is the hottest planet in our solar system," he said.

"Hotter than Mercury?" Cooper asked.

"Yep."

"You always know such interesting facts," Bella said. "How come?"

Rhino pointed to the books. "I read a lot." *Books first, baseball second.* Rhino's thinker always repeated that saying. It was the rule in their household.

"Think you'll play on Saturday?" Cooper asked. "The Groundhogs are a tough team. We need you back."

Rhino shook his head. "I'll be there, but I won't be of much use. The doctor says I'll probably be ready the week after."

"Hope so," Bella said. "Paul's the only other player we have at first base. He's a little clumsy."

"First base is hard," Rhino said. He'd struggled when he first switched to that position. Maybe Coach Ray would try another player there. Rhino knew that Paul didn't like the position. There was too much pressure for him.

First basemen had to field every kind of hit ball. Grounders, pop-ups, line drives. They had to handle long throws from the other players. In his short time playing the position, Rhino had learned to pay close attention to the base runners, and to be eagerly aware of every situation. He felt that he was in control of the infield, and he loved that. But he could see why it was so difficult for Paul.

Cooper was sitting on the edge of the couch, drumming his fingers on the table. "I need to go play some hoops," he said. "Sitting in school all day makes we want to explode."

"Me too," Bella said. "As soon as my dad gets home from work we're going to have a catch."

"Wish I could join you," Rhino said. He

stretched his toes and wiggled his ankle. It was stiff, but not too sore. "Guess I should walk around some more. Wish I could run. I have a *ton* of energy right now, but no way to use it."

If the ankle healed quickly, he might be able to practice next week. But that was a long time away. And Rhino wouldn't get to play in a game for twelve more days. That seemed like forever!

"Have fun out there!" he called as Bella and Cooper left. "I'll see you tomorrow at school."

Rhino would try to make the best of it. But he knew this would seem like the longest twelve days of his life.

· CHAPTER 3 ·
Using His Thinker

C.J. burst into the house a couple of hours later. "What a practice!" he said, flopping onto an armchair across from Rhino. "Coach had us running sprints all day. He said we haven't been quick enough on the base paths lately."

C.J. played shortstop base for his school's baseball team. He looked a lot like Rhino—lean and muscular, with short hair and a quick smile. He was bigger, of course. "I'm tired," he said, dropping his baseball glove to the floor.

"Lucky you," Rhino replied. "I'm not tired at all!"

"Sorry, little brother," C.J. said. "How's the ankle feeling?"

"Not bad."

"I know it stinks to be out with an injury," C.J. said. "It happens to all of us. Part of the game."

"The worst part," Rhino said.

C.J. shut his eyes and settled back in the chair. "Whew," he said softly. "I just want to stay here and not move." He pulled the brim of his orange baseball cap down low and let out a sigh.

Grandpa poked his head out from the kitchen. "Dinner's in fifteen minutes," he said. "C.J., I assume your clothes are nice and clean. Otherwise you wouldn't *think* of sitting in that chair."

C.J. stood up quickly. He made a funny face and wiped his hand over the seat, brushing off some loose dirt.

"Get yourself a shower. You're filthy," Grandpa said. He shook his head and turned to Rhino with a grin. He tapped his forehead. "Your brother's thinker must have turned off."

"That happens sometimes," Rhino said. "What are we eating?"

"Roast chicken. Rice. Corn and carrots." Grandpa laughed. "We would have had peas, but they went to a different use."

"They helped a lot," Rhino said. He lifted his foot. "Not much swelling left."

"You're taking good care of it," Grandpa said. "That's something to be proud of. A lot of players rush back from an injury—even a minor one—and only make it worse. Being patient with this will pay off, trust me."

At dinner, Rhino listened as C.J. talked about practice. "Coach said we would have won the other day if we'd hustled more. He's right."

"You always hustle," Rhino said. "I've never seen you let up for a second." Rhino played sports that way, too. All out, all the time.

C.J. set down his fork. "Not everybody does. Some players aren't as intense as we are."

"And that's okay, too," Grandpa said. "Sports are supposed to be fun."

"The hardest thing is not playing," Rhino added. "I'll feel pretty useless just sitting in the dugout on Saturday." He spooned some rice into his mouth and looked down at his plate.

"You can still help the team," Grandpa said. "Watch closely at next week's game. You might see some things that can help the other players."

"Like what?" Rhino asked.

"You never know," said C.J. "You might notice something about the pitcher. Maybe he always scratches his ear before he throws a curveball."

Rhino smiled and scratched his own ear. Then he reached for another piece of chicken.

"When I was in high school I had to miss an important basketball game," Grandpa said. He pushed back his chair and stood. "My toe was bruised so bad I couldn't run. But the coach told me to watch the other team's best player. I figured out that he had trouble driving to the left."

Grandpa crouched in a defensive position and leaned, hands up. "The key was to force him to go that way by cutting off the path to his right. I pointed that out to our guy who was covering him, and he shut him down in the second half."

Rhino thought that over. "You were like an assistant coach," he said. "I guess I could do that, too. It's not as good as playing, though."

"I think you'll be surprised what you notice when you watch the game and aren't caught up with playing. There's a lot more going on than you probably ever realized." Grandpa said as he sat back down in his chair.

Just be patient, Rhino's thinker said. *Let my ankle heal.*

"You'll learn some things that will make you a better player, too," Grandpa said. "Use your thinker to size up what you see. Let it really sink in."

"Your brain is an important piece of sports equipment," C.J. said. "I'm always thinking."

Grandpa cleared his throat. "Except when your thinker turns off."

C.J. laughed. "Sorry about the chair," he said. "I was *tired*, Grandpa! Hungry, too."

"No harm this time," Grandpa said. "You tracked in a lot of dirt, though. You can sweep that up after dinner."

Rhino fought back a smile. C.J. noticed. "I suppose your injury gets you out of your chores," C.J. said.

Rhino looked hopefully at Grandpa.

"You can do the dishes," Grandpa said. "You don't need your ankle for that."

Rhino grinned. He took another scoop of rice. "I'd better empty these dishes then," he said. "My appetite isn't injured, that's for sure."

· CHAPTER 4 ·
Left Out!

Cooper greeted Rhino with a high five as he entered the classroom. Rhino had only missed one day of school, but he was glad to be back.

"Let me show you something," Cooper said. He opened his desk and took out a pair of black-and-silver gloves. "My cousin gave them to me," Cooper said. "Batting gloves! I can't wait to use them at practice today."

The gloves had leather palms and stretchy fingers. They helped a player grip the bat tighter and absorbed some of the impact from hitting the ball.

"Very cool," Rhino said. "Like the pros wear."

"You can try them, too," Cooper said. "When you're ready to play, I mean."

Rhino frowned. He felt ready to play right now, but it would be at least a week until he could. Grandpa was going to drive him to practice after school so he could be with his team, but he couldn't help feeling left out.

He did his best to pay attention during math. Sometimes his mind drifted. He saw himself swinging the bat and smacking the ball deep into the outfield. It flew higher and higher. Over the fence for a home run!

Get back to Earth, his thinker told him. *Pay attention to the teacher.*

During reading class, Rhino felt his mind wandering again. This time he was planning out what he would say during the lunchtime conversation later in the day. Rhino was excited to tell his friends about the types of minerals that had been discovered on Mars. He glanced at the clock. Lunch was a long way off, and he was really looking forward to that astronomy talk. He'd be missing recess so he could ice his ankle.

I need to be responsible and take care of my foot, Rhino thought to himself. *I'll ice it at recess and meet my friends at lunch and it'll all be fine.* Rhino tried to pay attention to the rest of the lesson.

When recess time came, Rhino's classmates hurried out to the playground to play games. Rhino heard them chattering happily as he walked to the nurse's office. His ankle was a bit sore, but he didn't limp at all.

"Hello, Ryan," said the nurse, Mrs. Campbell. "I heard you had a little accident."

"It's not too bad," Rhino said. "The ice helps."

Mrs. Campbell put some ice cubes in a plastic bag. She placed a towel over Rhino's ankle and put the ice pack on it. Rhino had his reading book with him. He could get his homework assignment for tomorrow done now.

But he couldn't concentrate on the book. He saw himself racing around the bases after hitting the ball into the outfield. Then he made a great, diving catch on a line drive. Rhino played out every inning of an imaginary game in his mind. Of course, since it was his imagination, the Mustangs won easily. And Rhino hit a couple of very deep home runs.

The time passed quickly. When he heard the bell ring for the end of recess, Rhino hadn't read a single page even though he was holding the book open. He wanted to get back into that imaginary baseball game.

"I'll see you again at noon," Mrs. Campbell said.

"You will?"

"Yes," she said. "You're scheduled to ice the ankle again at lunchtime."

That was news to Rhino. He'd miss the astronomy discussion at the lunch table!

"I think my ankle is better," he said. "Maybe I can skip the icing."

"Oh, no," the nurse said. "The doctor said this is the last day for the ice, but you need to complete the process."

Rhino nodded. He knew that was the right thing to do.

But I'm being left out of everything! This stinks!

Rhino's classmates were coming in from recess. They didn't see him as he walked a few feet behind in the hallway.

"Wow, that was fun," said a girl.

"I'm sweating!" said Cooper. "That was a great game of tag."

Rhino's ankle felt numb from the ice. He loved tag. He loved *every* game on the playground.

An hour later, he was back in the nurse's office. He chewed his peanut-butter-and-jelly sandwich as he iced the ankle again. Even his favorite sandwich didn't taste so good today. His friends were having fun without him.

This is for the best—

Shut up, thinker!

Rhino let out a sigh. He sipped from his milk carton and stared at the ceiling. No baseball. No planet discussion. And he forgot to bring a bag of BBQ chips!

At least tomorrow things would start getting back to normal.

Okay, thinker. Let me have it.

This is for the best. Be patient. Be proud.

Be quiet!

Rhino began to smile. He liked arguing with his thinker sometimes, and he *was* proud. He was handling this setback like a grown-up. Being patient was hard, but he knew his ankle was getting better. He'd be ready next week.

Rhino passed Bella in the hallway. She raised her shoulders in a big shrug and asked, "Where were you?"

"Last session with the ice," Rhino said. "I'll be there tomorrow."

"You better be."

"What did you talk about?" Rhino asked. "The dust storms on Mars? Venus's volcanos?"

Bella laughed. "We talked about you!"

"Me?"

"Everyone felt bad that you were missing out," Bella said. "So we decided not to discuss the planets until you are back."

"Wow. That was nice of you."

"Everybody likes you, Rhino," Bella said. "When you and Cooper joined the group, it got more interesting. You always have something new to tell us."

Rhino felt his face grow warm. He looked down at his feet. "Thanks," he said.

"See you at practice?"

"I'll be there," Rhino replied. "I'll be stuck in the dugout, but I'll be there."

"Great," Bella said. "The Mustangs wouldn't be complete without you."

Bella hurried away to her classroom. Rhino lifted his right foot and gently flexed the ankle. No pain. Very little stiffness. It would be all better soon.

The hallway was empty. Rhino made two fists, as if he was gripping a baseball bat. He looked up the hall, imagining a pitcher forty-six feet away. He waited for the fastball. In his mind, he brought back the bat and swung.

Good-bye, Mr. Baseball, he thought. He could see the ball soaring over the center-field fence. He just had to wait a little longer.

· CHAPTER 5 ·
Eyes Open

Rhino touched the big white *M* on his baseball cap. Then he smelled the inside of the brim. The dried sweat reminded him how much he loved the game.

As Grandpa James drove into the parking lot, Rhino could see his teammates gathering on the field. It made him happy to see baseballs flying through the air.

"This is where I belong," Rhino said. "Thanks for bringing me."

"You're welcome," Grandpa said. "It's important to support your teammates, even if you can't play."

Rhino had to remind himself not to run from the car to the dugout. He would have to resist swinging a bat or throwing a ball to Cooper. It was all part of being patient.

Dylan stepped into the dugout and gave Rhino his wise-guy smile. "I've played with much worse injuries than that," he said, pointing to Rhino's foot. "You're being a wimp."

Dylan always managed to say something to annoy Rhino. They'd had plenty of arguments early in the season, but lately they'd been getting along. Dylan tried to pick on everyone.

"I'm just kidding," Dylan said. He ran his hand through his short blond hair. "I'm sure you'll play as soon as the boo-boo heals."

"I'm doing what the doctor told me to do," Rhino said. "And it's working! Can't you ever mind your own business?" Rhino was trying to be responsible by following the doctor's orders. The last thing he wanted to do was reinjure his ankle.

Dylan smacked his hand into his glove. "My

business is pitching," he said. He left the dugout and walked toward the mound.

What a pest, Rhino thought. Dylan was a very good player but not always a good teammate. Rhino had gotten into it with Dylan when he thought Dylan had stolen his bat. But it turned out Dylan was innocent and Ryan felt bad for accusing him with no evidence. Ever since then, Rhino tried to be more patient with Dylan, even though he still said the wrong thing sometimes.

Coach Ray had the Mustangs working on fielding today. He stood by home plate and hit ground balls to the infielders. After catching the ball, they threw it to first base.

Dylan stopped a sharp grounder and made the easy throw to Paul at first. Carlos did the same at second base. But when Cooper stabbed a hot grounder deep at shortstop, his long throw bounced in the dirt before reaching Paul.

Paul had his glove extended and his foot on the base. When the ball bounced, he leaned back, and the ball rose up and hit him in the arm. The same thing happened a few minutes later on a long throw from third. Both times, the ball rolled all the way to the fence.

"Don't be afraid of the ball!" Dylan yelled.

"I'm not afraid," Paul mumbled.

"Then catch it," Dylan said. He shook his head and frowned.

"Don't be such a poor sport," Rhino whispered, but nobody else heard it.

"Dylan," Coach Ray said sternly. "We're all learning here. It doesn't help to cut down your teammates."

"It's simple, Coach," Dylan said. "We field it. We throw it. He's supposed to catch it."

Make Dylan try playing first base, Rhino thought. *He'll see that it isn't as easy as he thinks.* But he didn't say anything. Coach Ray would make those decisions.

Rhino could see that backing away from a bouncing ball made it harder to catch. But he understood why Paul was doing it. When the ball was thrown in the air, it was easy to see where it was going. But a bounce in the dirt made its path harder to judge. Rhino had been hit with the ball a few times when it bounced in an unexpected direction.

"Hang in there, Paul!" Rhino called. "You're doing great and working hard."

Dylan rolled his eyes at Rhino.

Rhino held his tongue. *Don't stir up trouble on the team,* his thinker told him. Grandpa James always said to use your thinker before saying something out loud. But Rhino thought of himself as a leader of his teammates. He'd speak to Dylan when they were alone.

Coach continued the drill for about twenty more minutes. Paul caught nearly all of the accurate throws. He made a few good catches on wide throws or high ones. But he still had trouble when the ball bounced before it reached him. He bobbled a couple of easy ones and looked frustrated.

"Batting practice!" Coach called. "Dylan, Cooper, Carlos, come in to bat. I'll pitch today."

Dylan jogged to the dugout and put on a batting helmet.

"Make good contact," Rhino said. "Send one over the fence."

"Thanks. I plan to." Dylan picked up a bat and grinned.

"Wait a minute," Rhino said. "See what happened? I said something supportive. Felt good, huh?"

Dylan smirked. "I just want us to win," he said. "I'm not trying to be mean to Paul."

"Then say something helpful," Rhino replied. "Or nothing at all."

But Rhino wondered if *he* was being helpful. Could he help Paul play better? He'd have to think about that. He could tell Paul that he was doing great, but what good was that if Paul really wasn't?

Dylan was right about one thing. Paul would help the team if he managed to catch more of those throws.

Dylan's style was too harsh to be helpful. *But maybe my words were too soft,* Rhino thought. He needed something more useful to say to Paul. Something that would actually make him better at catching.

Rhino left the bench and leaned against the dugout fence. He watched what the infielders did with every hit ball. He focused on what Paul did when he tried to catch their throws. He studied Paul's footwork and noticed how often he backed away from the ball. Paul seemed more interested in protecting himself from getting hit than actually making the play.

I never would have noticed those things if I was out on the field, Rhino thought. *Maybe a few days away from the action is a good thing after all.*

Rhino was starting to get some ideas. He'd made many of those same mistakes himself. Grandpa and C.J. had helped him learn the right way to make the play. Maybe they could help him help Paul.

· CHAPTER 6 ·
Short Hops

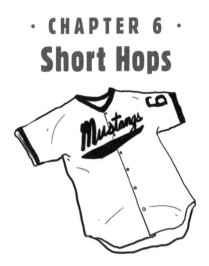

It was pizza night! Grandpa and Rhino drove to the middle school to pick up C.J., and they headed to Roman's.

"We'll eat at home," Grandpa said. "I phoned in the order earlier. And I made a big salad."

The café was very busy, but their pizza was ready. Rhino waved to a girl from his class who was seated at a booth with her parents. An old rock 'n' roll song was playing, and red candles flickered on the tabletops.

Rhino's mouth watered all the way home. The smell of pizza crust and cheese and tomato sauce filled the car. He lifted the lid just a little and inhaled. "Awesome," he said.

"Don't touch!" Grandpa said with a laugh. "No picking at the crust."

Rhino grabbed two slices as soon as he sat down at the dining room table. "I didn't think I'd build such an appetite sitting in the dugout," he joked.

"You boys are always ready to eat," Grandpa said. "But have some salad before you take any more pizza. And I have a special surprise for dessert."

Rhino scooped the mix of lettuce and tomatoes onto his plate. Grandpa had added some olives and green peas.

"Uh-oh," said C.J from across the table. "Those aren't the peas Rhino had on his foot all weekend are they?"

"Ha!" Grandpa said. "What's a little foot odor?"

C.J. raised his eyebrows.

"Rest easy," Grandpa said. "I threw the ankle peas away. We froze and re-froze those twenty times.

They turned into jelly by the time Little Rhino was finished with them." Grandpa smiled. "You boys stay here while I go take care of something in the kitchen."

When Grandpa was gone, Rhino told C.J. about Paul's troubles at first base. "He seems afraid of the ball when it bounces in the dirt."

"Ah, the short hop," C.J. said. "Throws in the dirt are tough to judge. The trick is to watch the ball closely so you can read the bounce. Get as close to it as you can. That way, you catch it on the way up, but before it gets too high. You keep your glove open and move it toward the ball."

Rhino nodded. He'd figured some of that out by watching.

"Look," C.J. said. "I'll demonstrate." He bounced a pea off the wooden table and it hit Rhino in the chest. "You weren't ready for that. Bounce one at me."

Rhino looked toward the kitchen. Grandpa was still in there. Rhino threw a pea hard, bouncing it in the middle of the table. C.J. jutted his hand forward and stopped it with his palm. "See, I met the ball while it was rising. I controlled it. Try another."

Rhino's second pea splatted on the table. It left a smudge of green.

"You need a firmer one," C.J. said. "Try again."

Rhino picked through his salad bowl. He held a pea between two fingers and decided that it was rubbery enough.

This pea bounced. C.J. caught it and closed his fist around it.

"You have quick reflexes," Rhino said. "But a baseball is a lot harder. When you get hit with one, it stings."

"That's true," C.J. said. "So you have to get your glove on it. You have to catch that ball before it catches you."

"Right." Rhino eyed the pizza box. There were three slices left, but Grandpa had eaten only one.

He'd probably want two more. Maybe Rhino could split the last piece with C.J.

C.J. howled as a pea hit Rhino's cheek. "Where are your reflexes?" he asked.

"No fair," Rhino said. He wiped the pea away with his thumb and winced. "I was looking at the pizza."

"Expect the unexpected," C.J. said. He fired another pea toward Rhino. And at that second, Grandpa came back into the room.

"Nice aim," Grandpa said. "Is that what we do with our food?"

"I . . . I was showing Rhino something," C.J. said. "For baseball."

"I see," Grandpa said. "Throwing a curveball with a pea?"

"It was about fielding," C.J. replied.

"It's true," Rhino said. "He was teaching me how to field a short hop."

Grandpa stared at the smashed pea on the table. He shook his head and laughed. "You boys sure are

amusing. From now on, do your baseball playing out in the yard. With a *baseball.* Got it?"

"Got it," both boys replied.

Grandpa sat down with a bag.

"C.J., you can vacuum the dining room tonight," Grandpa said. "And don't grind any loose peas into the carpet."

C.J. nodded.

Rhino cut a pizza slice in half and peeled it out of the box. "Thanks for the tip," he said to C.J.

"After dinner, we'll work on short hops in the yard," Grandpa said. "You watch C.J. and me. You'll learn a lot more than bouncing peas."

"Great!" Rhino said. "So . . . what is in the bag?"

Grandpa pulled out a tub of chocolate chip cookie dough ice cream and a small container of sprinkles. "With all of this talk of icing feet, I figured we could ice our stomachs with some of this!"

· CHAPTER 7 ·
Fact Finders

Rhino couldn't believe what he saw in the cafeteria the next day at lunchtime. His friends had made a poster that said WELCOME BACK, RHINO! Someone had drawn a picture of him riding a giant T. rex.

Rhino was smiling ear to ear as he took his seat at the table. He was so happy to be back with his lunch group. "Dinosaurs or planets today?" he asked.

"Planets," said Bella. "We know you've been waiting for that."

Rhino took out his PB&J sandwich. He had read more about Mars after doing his homework last night. He had lots of great information to share.

"What do you think Martians look like?" asked Kerry, a girl with long black braids. She usually led the discussions.

"I dressed up as a Martian last Halloween," said a boy with round glasses. "I had a big green mask with giant eyes and antennas."

"I think they'd look more like us," said Bella. "Maybe smaller and with squeaky voices."

Rhino knew that finding human-like beings on Mars was very unlikely. "If there's life on Mars, it's probably microscopic," he said. "Very tiny."

"That's no fun," said Kerry. "Why can't they be like us?"

"Mars is too cold," Rhino said. "And too dry. Not enough oxygen. Scientists have been exploring Mars for years with robotic probes. They haven't found any signs of life like us."

"Maybe they live in caves," Cooper said.

"Maybe," Rhino said. "Or way under the

ground. But if there are any living creatures there, they probably live in the ice at the poles. And they'd still be tiny. Like bacteria here on Earth."

The other kids looked at each other. Rhino shrugged. He didn't want to disappoint his friends, but he knew a lot about Mars. "Those are the facts," he said.

"No purple monsters up there?" Cooper asked.

Rhino laughed. "No, but it's still a very interesting place," he said. "Mars has two moons. And the gravity is so weak you could jump ten feet into the air."

"I want to go there," Cooper said. "Jumping that high would be awesome."

"Dress warm," Rhino replied. "The temperature is always below freezing."

The boy with the round glasses spoke up. "Everybody talks about Martians as if they go around in flying saucers." He tapped his finger on the table. "Let's stick to reality in this group."

"Agreed," said Kerry. "I read something cool. If Earth was the size of a basketball, Mars would be like a softball."

"Sounds about right," Rhino said. "And Venus is almost exactly the same size as Earth. Slightly smaller, like a soccer ball."

The talk quickly switched to Venus. Rhino decided that he'd said enough, so he chewed his PB&J sandwich and listened. It was so great to be back. His friends were funny and very curious about the world. These discussions had become a highlight of his school days.

I like this as much as recess, Rhino thought. "We need a name for this group," he said. "Like the Reality Team or something."

"How about the Truth Company?" said Cooper.

"Or Explorer . . . something," said Bella. "Explorer Squad?"

"That sounds like a hiking club," said Kerry. "It has to be a name that says what we are."

Rhino had another idea. He listened to it a couple of times in his head. It sounded right. He took a big sip from his milk carton and looked around. "The Fact Patrol," he said.

Everybody liked that one.

"We should get T-shirts with FACT PATROL printed on them," Cooper said as they walked back to class.

"Cool idea," Rhino said.

"Or baseball caps," Cooper said. "With *FP*, like our *M* for Mustangs."

"Yeah." Rhino had forgotten about baseball during lunchtime. That didn't happen very often. "Speaking of caps, do you think I should wear my uniform to the game on Saturday?"

"Why not?" Cooper asked.

"You know I can't play."

"Wear it," Cooper said. "You're still a team member. Don't even think about not suiting up."

Rhino was glad to hear that. He was so proud to wear his jersey with the big number 6. "What do the major leaguers do when they're injured?" Rhino asked.

"I think it depends how long they'll be out of action," Cooper said. "You'll only miss one game. We want to see you right there with us. Part of the team all the way."

"Maybe I should dress up like a mustang," Rhino said, laughing. "The team mascot!"

Cooper shook his head. "Funny idea, but I'd rather see you in uniform."

"I was kidding," Rhino said. "You know how serious I am about baseball."

"So am I."

"I want to be a major leaguer someday," Rhino said. "Missing one game won't stop me. And if that doesn't work out, maybe I'll be a scientist. An astronomer or a fossil hunter!"

"You can be both," Cooper said. "Me too!"

"Reach for the stars," Rhino said.

For now, he'd concentrate on baseball. But he was even more excited than ever about the Fact Patrol.

· CHAPTER 8 ·
Pressure!

Saturday was cloudy but warm. Rhino walked quickly to the field. His ankle didn't hurt at all.

There was a game going on when he arrived, so he sat in the bleachers with Cooper. "When we warm up, will you help me show Paul a few things?" Rhino asked.

"Sure. But I thought you weren't supposed to throw or catch yet."

"I won't," Rhino said. "But I want to give him some tips about those short hops. If you throw him a few hot ones, I'll try to guide him through it."

On the field, the batter hit a hard line drive

deep into left field. Two runners scored, and the Sharks celebrated another win.

"That's two wins in a row for them," Cooper said. "They beat us in the last inning a week ago."

"I think they're in first place," Rhino said. "But we're pretty close. You guys need to get us a win today."

Cooper stood near second base, and Paul lined up at first. "Put every throw in the dirt," Rhino said. "Throw it close to Paul, but make that ball jump."

Rhino told Paul what he'd learned from C.J. and Grandpa. "Try not to back away," he said. "Move your glove toward the ball."

Paul missed a few and got hit in the shoulder with one bounce, but he began to get the hang of it. Soon he was catching most of the throws.

"Thanks, Coach Rhino!" Paul said with a laugh. "I still hope you get back in the game in a hurry, but I think I can handle first base today."

Rhino cheered harder than he ever had before. Each time the Mustangs got a base runner, he yelled for him to score. When Dylan struck out three Groundhogs in a row, Rhino met him at the edge of the dugout and gave him a high five.

But neither team was able to score. The game was tied 0–0 after two innings, after three, after four.

"We could use your power today," Bella said to Rhino as the Mustangs batted in the top of the fifth. "One of your home runs would make all the difference."

Rhino nodded. "Wish I could."

Rhino did everything he could to help the team. He handed out water bottles when the players came off the field. He told Cooper to be a bit more patient at bat and not swing at outside pitches. And he continued to encourage Paul. So far Paul had handled all of the throws and fielded a few ground balls. But none of those plays had been hard to make.

Finally, in the sixth inning, Cooper reached third base with a triple. A minute later, Bella rapped a single up the middle to drive Cooper home.

Rhino made a fist and shouted, "Yeah!" Cooper burst into the dugout, panting and sweaty. "Three more outs and we'll win this game," he said. "I didn't know if we could do that without you."

"Sure we can," Rhino said. *But we'll be even better when I get back,* he thought. *Maybe we can win the league championship.*

As the Groundhogs came up to bat, Rhino couldn't sit still. He stood behind the dugout fence. He could smell hot dogs and french fries cooking at the refreshment stand. He was hoping to dig into that as soon as his teammates finished this victory.

For now, his focus was on the field. Dylan threw a few warm-up pitches. The infielders tossed a ball "around the horn," from one player to another.

Rhino was more nervous watching than he would have been on the field. *At least I'd be in control*

of things out there, he thought. All he could do now was watch and cheer.

Dylan struck out the first batter, but then things got tough. He walked the next one, and the Groundhogs' pitcher hit the ball over Cooper's head for a single. The other runner advanced to third.

Yikes, Rhino thought. This felt too much like last week's game, when the Mustangs lost in the final inning. He glanced at Paul, who looked glum. Unless Dylan got a couple more strikeouts, there might be some tough plays ahead.

"Let's go, Dylan!" Rhino shouted.

The pressure increased as Dylan threw a strike and two balls. Rhino kicked at the dirt. His mouth felt dry.

Crack! The batter lined the ball straight toward second base. It took a high bounce just past the pitcher's mound, and it looked like it would be a base hit.

Cooper was ready at shortstop. He darted into the gap behind second base and nabbed the ball. He flipped it to Carlos, who stepped on second base for one out and swung around to throw to first.

The runner from third slid into home. That would tie the game, but the run would not count if the Mustangs could complete the double play.

The throw to first base was wild. Paul lunged to his left and the ball took a dreaded short hop in front of him. But Paul didn't back away. He drove his glove toward the ball, scooped it up, and turned to tag the batter.

"Out!" called the umpire.

The Mustangs had won!

Rhino ran onto the field to join his teammates, who were surrounding Paul. Cooper slapped Paul on the back and whooped. Bella was sprinting in from right field with her arms raised. Even Dylan was jumping up and down and yelling.

Paul grabbed Rhino's arm and pulled him toward him. "I never would have made that catch without your help," he said. "Thanks!"

"You did it yourself," Rhino said. "Great job."

"Not bad for my *last* play at first base," Paul said with a giant grin. "It's all yours next week."

"I don't know," Rhino replied. "You were the player of the game today."

"I can do without that pressure," Paul said. "I'll be much happier out in center field."

Rhino didn't think he could be any happier. He wanted to play, but he also felt so good about seeing his teammates win.

In just a few days he'd be able to practice again. He was certain that the Mustangs would be the best team in the league when he was back in the lineup.

· CHAPTER 9 ·
Almost Ready

At recess on Monday, Rhino tossed a rubber ball back and forth with Cooper. His ankle felt as good as new, but Grandpa told him not to run or jump yet. Rhino thought back to the painful moment when he had twisted the ankle. Could it happen again?

He watched the other kids playing tag and climbing on the playground equipment. He wanted to join them. *At least I'm doing something athletic*, Rhino thought. He'd missed an entire week of recess. He knew that he'd be able to take part in baseball practice the next afternoon.

"Toss that here!" yelled a friendly voice.

Rhino turned to see Bella trotting toward him. He threw the ball and she jumped to catch it.

"My birthday is next week," Bella said. "We're having a team party after practice tomorrow to celebrate. It will be at the baseball field. At the picnic tables. Cake, hot dogs, stuff like that."

"Awesome," Rhino said. He'd ask Grandpa to help him pick out a present.

"Are you ready?" Bella asked.

"For baseball? I'm always ready." But Rhino hadn't swung a bat since the injury occurred. He hoped that there was nothing wrong with his ankle that would make it likely to get hurt often. He had read that one ankle injury sometimes led to another.

Rhino lifted his foot and turned it in a circle. Then he turned it the other way. He flexed his foot up and down. "It seems perfect," he said. "We'll find out tomorrow."

"Easy does it, according to my dad," Bella said. "He told me he wanted to ease you back into things."

"That's what I'm doing," Rhino said. "Throwing a little today. Batting a little tomorrow. By Saturday, I'll be all the way back." *I hope.*

Rhino knew that thinking about the ankle would not help him at all when he tried to bat. He'd need to relax his mind and swing normally. Worrying about what might happen would probably keep him from concentrating on the pitch. It would make him strike out.

Rhino blew out his breath. "I'll be ready," he said, nodding slowly. "And I can't wait!"

Rhino thought about batting all afternoon. That evening, he asked if he could swing his bat a few times in the yard. Grandpa agreed.

"I don't think I could sleep tonight if I wasn't sure about my ankle," Rhino said.

Grandpa smiled and put his hand on Rhino's shoulder. "No pitching," Grandpa said. "Just take a few regular swings. That will set your mind at ease. The injury was a fluke, but we'll be extra careful for now."

"I'll help," C.J. said. "I'm an expert batting coach!"

They hurried out to the yard.

Grandpa told Rhino to make his normal swing a few times. Rhino imagined a home plate at his feet. He brought back his bat and looked out to about where the pitcher's mound would be.

Rhino lifted his right foot slightly as he swung the bat. He stepped that foot forward and made a nice, smooth swing.

"Good," Grandpa said. "It looked as if you stepped a bit out of line, though. Let's see it again."

"I saw it!" C.J. said after the second swing. "Step straight forward, Rhino. And no more than six inches."

Rhino swung again, making sure to step straight ahead.

"Do you think that's why I got hurt?" he asked. "From stepping to the side?"

Grandpa shook his head. "Probably not. But it's important to do things right when you swing."

C.J. reached for the bat. C.J. was left-handed, too, so he had his right foot forward when he batted. "Watch," he said. He went through the proper steps. "Every time you practice a sports skill, you want to do it the right way. Think about shooting free throws in basketball. To be good at that, you have to use the same motion, every time. Same thing with batting."

C.J. swung again. "*Consistency.* That's the key. No matter what sport I play, the coaches always say to do things the right way, every time." He handed the bat to Rhino.

"Just a few more swings," Grandpa said. "Does the ankle feel all right?"

"Perfect," Rhino said. He swung three more times.

"You've got it," C.J. said.

Rhino gripped his bat tighter. He loved how solid the wood felt. Just right for him.

I'll hit a home run on Saturday, he thought. *Maybe two!* But he was happy just to be getting ready to play again. It had been a long wait.

Consistency. His thinker would help him remember that. He knew that lots of practice would make him succeed. Not just in the next game, but for his entire sports career.

I'll restart this season in a big way on Saturday, he thought. *Bring it on, I'm ready!*

· CHAPTER 10 ·
Fun Time

Rhino hurried to the field on Tuesday. He was carrying the present for Bella's party, wrapped in golden paper.

First, he had baseball business to take care of. He was *so* ready for this after the long layoff. *The wait was worth it,* his thinker said. *Be grateful for this chance. It's smooth sailing ahead!*

Rhino fielded a dozen ground balls, then caught a few high pops. Coach Ray decided to have the infielders work on double plays.

"We turned a great double play in that last game," he said. "We wouldn't have won without it.

But if Paul hadn't made that tough catch and the tag, it would have been a different story."

Everyone got involved. There was a base runner on first, and another one to run from home plate to first. Coach hit the ball to either the shortstop or the second baseman. The one who didn't get the ball covered second, and then made the throw to first.

Rhino and Paul took turns playing first base. Paul groaned, but he was a good sport about it. "There's a great song, Coach," Paul said. "It's called 'Centerfield.' Ever hear it? It goes, 'Look at me, I can be . . . center field.'"

Coach winked at Paul. "Of course I've heard that song! Don't worry, Paul. Rhino will go back to being our regular first baseman. But everybody needs a back-up, just in case."

The action was very quick. Every runner wanted to beat the throw to second, and sometimes they did.

Rhino took a turn, too. "Watch this," he said to

Paul. "I'll be at that base before Cooper even gets to the ball."

As Coach hit the ball, Rhino sprinted toward second. He slid into the base just as Carlos took the throw from Cooper. Carlos pivoted and threw it to Paul.

"Did I make it?" Rhino asked, kneeling on the base.

"I'm not sure," Coach said. "What does everybody think?"

Everybody yelled at once. "Safe!" "Out!" "Safe!"

"Out, out, out!" Cooper called. He jutted his thumb toward the dugout and laughed.

"We need an umpire!" Rhino said, grinning at Cooper. "I think I was safe by a mile." Rhino was always serious during a game, but joking around a little in practice seemed okay. This was one of the best parts of baseball. Grandpa always said to have fun.

"Can I try again?" Rhino asked.

"That's enough sliding for you today," Coach

said. "No more until the game. Let's make sure that ankle stays in tip-top shape."

Rhino took another turn playing first base. They were successful in making the double play about half the time.

"That's it for today!" Coach Ray called. "Great workout. Time to enjoy the party."

They walked to the picnic tables near the field and sang "Happy Birthday" to Bella. Her mom had set it up with tablecloths and cupcakes. She had hot dogs cooking on a grill.

Bella smiled when she unwrapped the gift from Rhino. "The Big Book of Planets," she read from the cover. "Maybe now I can keep up with you at lunchtime!"

Rhino licked some chocolate cupcake frosting from his finger. "I'm way ahead of you," he said.

"You probably memorized the whole book," Bella said. "But I'll learn. I'm a Fact Patrol member, too."

All of the players had nice gifts for Bella. Even Dylan gave her a box of chocolates.

Rhino loaded up a hot dog with mustard and relish. Cooper had so much cupcake in his mouth that he couldn't talk. Paul was making a big stack of potato chips, stuck together with ketchup. Even small, quiet Carlos was joking about one of his wild throws that soared over the fence.

This is a great thing about baseball, too, Rhino thought. *Being part of a team.* He had made several new friends this season.

Baseball was even better than he'd hoped it would be.

· CHAPTER 11 ·
Back in the Game

Rhino ran all the way to the field on Saturday morning. He had so much energy that he knew he wouldn't get tired out.

Watch out, everybody, he thought. *Here comes Number 6!*

"Our team is complete again!" Bella yelled when she saw him.

"Nobody can stop us now," said Cooper.

Rhino slapped hands with Carlos. He gave Paul a high five. During warm-ups, he caught every ball that came his way. During batting practice, he lined several pitches into the outfield.

He was excited! The Mustangs were facing the Tigers for the second time this season. The Tigers had a fast pitcher named Chang, but Rhino had hit a game-winning home run the first time. He couldn't wait to get up there again.

But Rhino was shocked to discover that he wasn't in the starting lineup.

"I'm not sure you're ready to play a full game," Coach Ray told him. "You'll get in there later, but let's take it slow."

Paul looked toward the sky. "I hoped I'd never see first base again," he said. He laughed and walked onto the field.

"I'm ready, Coach," Rhino said softly.

"I know," Coach replied. "But let's play it safe for one more game."

Stay patient, Rhino's thinker told him. But it was hard.

The Mustangs were locked in another tight game. They were tied 1–1 in the third inning. The Tigers had two outs. Rhino knew he would start playing in the fourth inning, so he began to stretch.

Dylan walked two batters in a row. "Settle down!" Rhino called.

The next batter hit Dylan's first pitch high over the fence in center field. Home run. Suddenly, the Tigers had a 4–1 lead.

After a groundout ended the inning, the Mustangs trotted quietly to the dugout.

"Let's show some spirit!" Rhino yelled. "We'll get those runs back."

Dylan threw his glove onto the bench and sat down in a huff.

"Is your arm okay?" Coach asked him.

Dylan stared straight ahead for a moment. He sighed. "It's kind of tired, I guess. A little bit sore."

"No problem," Coach said. "We'll move you to shortstop. Cooper will pitch."

"What about me?" Rhino asked.

"You'll pinch-hit for Paul if he gets to bat

this inning," Coach said. "Then you can go in at first base."

Paul was scheduled to be the Mustangs' fourth batter. As long as someone got on base, Rhino would bat in his place.

"Guess I'm finally done at first base," Paul said.

"You handled it great," Rhino replied. "Nice work."

Dylan drew a walk with two outs, and Rhino stepped toward the plate. He thought about the home runs he'd hit earlier in the season.

But he also thought about what happened last time he batted in a game. Pain!

That was two whole weeks ago, his thinker told him. *The ankle's healed! Just connect with that pitch.*

He went over the things Grandpa and C.J. had told him. *Step straight ahead. Swing smoothly.*

"Let's go, Chang!" yelled the shortstop.

The Tigers' pitcher narrowed his eyes and stared at Rhino. He was tall, and he pitched with a quick, overhand release.

The first pitch looked great to Rhino. It was a little high and a little outside, but it was straight and not very fast.

Rhino swung hard.

The ball smacked into the catcher's glove.

"Strike!" called the umpire.

Rhino wiggled his toes. *How did I miss that?* He took a practice swing and got ready.

The next pitch was inside and faster. Rhino leaned back as it went by.

"Strike two!"

The Tigers cheered and pounded their gloves. Rhino tapped the plate with his bat. He couldn't let another close pitch get past.

Whoosh. His swing hit nothing. The Tigers ran off the field. Rhino walked slowly to the dugout to get his glove.

"Three seconds," came a steady voice. Rhino looked up to see Grandpa James in the bleachers. They both smiled. The three-second rule meant that you could feel bad about a mistake for that long, but then you had to get over it.

"Keep your head up," Coach Ray told him. "You're just a little rusty."

Rhino nodded. He ran to first base and threw a ball to Carlos.

Cooper pitched very well and didn't allow any runs. But the Mustangs still trailed, 4–1. They needed a rally. In the sixth inning, they started one.

Cooper singled. Bella did, too. When Dylan drew another walk, the bases were loaded for Rhino.

It was easy to do the math. A home run would win the game. *Grand slam,* Rhino thought. *Bash that ball and make it happen.*

But his thinker knew better. *Just connect,* it told him. *Any hit will bring in some runs.*

The pitcher glared at Rhino. Rhino glared back.

The pitch was fast and straight down the middle.

Crack! Rhino was running as soon as the ball left his bat. It dropped into the gap between left field and center, and rolled all the way to the fence.

Cooper scored. Bella did, too. Dylan rounded third and raced toward home as the shortstop caught the throw from the center fielder.

"Slide, Dylan!" yelled a Mustang.

Rhino kept running.

Dylan slid and a cloud of dust flew into the air.

"Safe!" yelled the umpire.

Rhino dove into third base. The game was tied. Everyone else was on their feet, yelling and jumping.

Rhino stood, too. He took a deep breath and wiped the dirt from the front of his jersey. His work wasn't done yet.

Carlos came up to bat. He was an excellent fielder, but he didn't have many hits this season.

Just put it in the outfield, Rhino thought. *I'll score.*

Carlos popped the first pitch high into the air. The first baseman ran toward it, but it drifted into foul territory.

Carlos put some power behind the next one. It flew in the air into right field. Rhino kept one foot firmly on third base. Since there were no outs yet, he could run as soon as the ball was caught. It would be a race against the throw. If he scored, it would mean a win for the Mustangs.

The outfielder caught the ball. Rhino put his head down and pumped his arms, sprinting with all of his speed.

The cheering from the crowd rose in one giant "Ohhhhhh!"

The catcher squatted squarely in front of home plate. Here came the ball! Here came Rhino!

He heard the *smack* of the ball in the catcher's glove. He felt the plate a half a second before he felt the tag on his leg.

"Safe!" was the call.

The catcher groaned.

Rhino leaped up. His teammates were racing toward him.

Back in business, Rhino thought. He flexed his ankle and it felt great.

The hugs from his teammates felt even better. The Mustangs had won again.

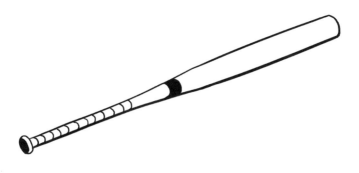

LET THE GAME BEGIN!

SEE WHERE IT ALL STARTED IN BOOK #1!

Little Rhino stepped up to home plate. He gripped the bat tight. The breeze in the treetops sounded like the crowd at a Major League Baseball game. He imagined that the bases were loaded.

Hit this one out of the park, he told himself.

Rhino glared at the pitcher. Here came the ball!

With a hard, steady swing, Rhino connected. The smack of the bat against the ball sent a thrill through his body.

"Nice hit!" said Grandpa James with a smile.

Rhino smiled back. He dropped the plastic bat and watched as the ball flew over the tall hedge. He'd hit it out of the backyard! Rhino had never hit one that far before.

Grandpa pitched to Rhino every day after Rhino's homework was done. "Books first, baseball second" was the rule in their house. Rhino always raced home from third grade, had a snack, and did his work. Then he changed into shorts and an oversized jersey, grabbed his bat and glove, and met Grandpa in the yard.

"You're really hitting them now, Rhino," Grandpa said. Rhino's real name was Ryan but everyone except his teachers used his nickname. "Better get that ball before it rolls all the way to Main Street!"

Rhino laughed. He knew the ball hadn't gone that far. It was just a plastic one—not like the real MLB baseball they used for playing catch. He hit with a plastic one because a real one might break a window. That would be bad.

Rhino trotted out of the yard. He stopped cold when he saw Dylan on the other side of the street. Dylan was tall and thin and always looked mean. He was holding Rhino's ball.

"Looking for this?" Dylan said with a sneer. "Come and get it, wimp."

Rhino gulped. Dylan was the meanest kid in third grade. He teased everyone and often got into fights. *Dylan acts tough, but he's not,* Rhino's thinker said. Grandpa James would always point to his head and say, "Your thinker is there to think the things you can't say out loud."

Still, Dylan was bigger than Rhino. He was always sneering, his glasses sitting crooked on his face, and his stiff blond hair stood up on his head, making him look even taller.

"Come on over," Dylan said. "Come get your baby ball."

Rhino looked back. The leafy hedge blocked Grandpa's view. Rhino couldn't return to the backyard without the ball. He swallowed hard and walked across the street.

Rhino reached for the ball. Dylan held out his hand, then pulled it away. Rhino reached again. Dylan twisted and waved the ball over his head.

"Give me the ball," Rhino said. Inside his head, his thinker added, *You big bully.*

Dylan held the ball out again. "Take it," he said.

Rhino put his hand on the ball. Dylan wouldn't let go.

"Let me have it," Rhino said. *This is why you have zero friends, Dylan,* he thought. *You're nothing but a big-mouthed bully.*

"Just take it," Dylan said. But he gripped the ball harder.

Rhino frowned and squinted his brown eyes. He pulled the ball, but Dylan just laughed. He was stronger than Rhino.

Rhino heard Grandpa's voice from the yard. "Rhino?" he said. "Is everything all right?"

Dylan looked surprised when he heard Rhino's grandfather. He yanked the ball away, then threw it at Rhino. It hit Rhino's chest and fell to the street. Rhino scooped it up.

Dylan was walking away fast. Rhino had never seen Dylan back down from something before. He didn't look back.

Rhino stepped into the yard. Grandpa James had come closer to the hedge. He raised his bushy eyebrows but didn't say anything.

Rhino felt shaky. He didn't like uncomfortable situations. If Grandpa hadn't been there, Dylan might have started a fight. Or he might have kept the ball.

"Ready to hit some more?" Grandpa said. He gripped an imaginary bat, flexing his arm muscles, and making a powerful swing. Grandpa had always been very fit and athletic.

Rhino slowly walked back over to Grandpa. "I think I've had enough for today," he said softly.

"Really?" Grandpa asked. "You usually want to hit until it gets dark out."

Rhino shrugged. "I guess I'm tired." He felt embarrassed because Dylan had picked on him and Rhino didn't get a chance to stand up for himself. He had let his thinker do all of his arguing, and then his grandfather showed up. Grandpa James probably heard the whole thing.

Grandpa put his hand on Rhino's shoulder. "Three seconds," he said.

Grandpa had taught Rhino the "three second

rule." When you're angry or feeling bad about your-self, take three seconds to be upset. Then remember how great you are.

Rhino let his shoulders drop. He blew out his breath.

"Let's do some throwing," Grandpa said. He picked up a hardball and watched Rhino grab his glove off the lawn.

"Sounds good," Rhino said. After a few throws he felt better.

Grandpa tossed the ball high in the air. Pop flies like those were the hardest ones for Rhino to catch. The daylight was fading. Rhino set him-self under the ball and watched as it reached its highest point. The ball seemed to hang in midair for a second. Then it dropped. Rhino made the catch.

"Nice one," Grandpa said.

Last month, when they'd started practicing baseball, Rhino almost never caught a pop fly. Now he grabbed them every time.

"You've made a lot of progress," Grandpa said. "Everything takes time and practice. Catching pop-ups. Hitting the ball."

Rhino nodded. Then he remembered the clash with Dylan. He stared toward the hedge and replayed the conflict. *I should have told him to get lost,* he thought.

"Everything takes time, Little Rhino," Grandpa said again. "Even dealing with a bully."

YOU CAN'T HIT WITHOUT A BAT!

HERE'S A LOOK BACK AT BOOK #2!

*B*ring it on, Little Rhino thought.

Baseball season was here! Rhino and his teammates had been practicing for two weeks. Finally, Saturday's game would be for real.

Rhino hit a game-winning home run in the Mustangs' practice game a few days earlier. He'd also made a great catch in center field. He felt confident. He was ready. Today's practice session was the last one before the opener.

"I'm going to smack another homer," Rhino said. "My new bat is awesome."

The bat was a gift from Grandpa James. He had surprised Rhino with it that morning. "You earned this," Grandpa said. Rhino had received excellent grades on his latest progress report. He worked just as hard in the classroom as he did on the baseball field. Rhino was so happy. The bat felt perfect when he swung it—almost like it was part of his body. It was the right weight and length for him, and it cut smoothly through the air.

The day was warm and sunny. Rhino pulled off his sweatshirt. He untucked his baggy white T-shirt out from his shorts. The team didn't practice in their uniforms. Then Rhino wrapped his hoodie around the new bat he had with him and set it on the dugout bench. He and his best friend Cooper were the first players to arrive at the field, as usual.

"Let's catch, Rhino," Cooper said. "We need to warm up." "Rhino" was the nickname that everyone called him, even though his real name was Ryan.

They tossed a ball back and forth. Coach Ray and his daughter, Bella, arrived a minute later. Other players started to trickle in, too. They were all wearing their bright blue caps with the big *M* for Mustangs.

Bella trotted over and winked at Rhino. "Hey, Cooper," she said, flipping her brown ponytail. "Mind if we switch? I need to work with my outfield partner." Bella had played right field in the practice game.

"Sure," Cooper replied. He looked around for someone else to throw with.

Bella punched her glove and said, "Fire it here, Rhino." She had her cap on backward.

After everyone had warmed up, Coach started a drill. "We need to develop quick hands," he said. He had one player in each group send a fast ground ball to the other.

"Field it cleanly, then release it fast," Coach said. "A quick throw can make the difference between an out and a base runner."

They worked on that for several minutes, then Coach sent the starters out to their positions. It was time for batting practice. "Play it like a real game," Coach said. "Run out every hit. You'll all get plenty of chances to swing the bat today."

Rhino sprinted to center field. He was so excited that he hopped up and down, waiting to make his first catch of the day.

He didn't wait long. The first batter looped a soft fly ball over the head of the second baseman. It looked like it would drop for a single, but Rhino darted after it.

The ball hung in the air just long enough for Rhino to get under it. He reached out his glove on the run and made the catch, then tossed the ball back to the pitcher.

"Incredible speed," said Bella, who had run over to back him up. "No one's going to get a hit if you're out here!"

Rhino blushed. *What's up with Bella lately being all nicey nice?* He trotted back to his position.

He caught another fly ball and fielded two grounders that got through for singles. Then Coach waved the three outfielders in to bat.

Rhino put on a helmet and grabbed his new bat. He stood with Bella while their teammate named Carlos took his turn at the plate. Carlos was the smallest player on the team but he was a good fielder.

"Nice bat," Bella said to Rhino. "Brand-new?"

Rhino nodded. "It's the best bat," he said. He handed it to Bella for a look.

"Too heavy," Bella said.

"It's just right for me," Rhino replied.

Rhino studied the pitcher. Dylan was a wise guy and often a bully, but he was a good athlete. He'd given Rhino a hard time early in the season, but lately he minded his own business.

I still don't trust him but he is *my teammate.* Rhino's thinker said. Grandpa had taught Rhino to always use his head and think things through.

Dylan took off his cap and ran his hand through his blond hair. He smirked at the batter, put his cap back on, and wound up to pitch.

Carlos swung and missed. Dylan laughed. His next pitch was a strike, too. Carlos finally hit a weak ground ball that Dylan fielded. His throw to first was a little high, and it bounced off the first baseman's glove and dropped to the ground.

"Don't be afraid of the ball!" Dylan yelled at the first baseman, Paul.